Kevin Garnett

A Basketball Star Who Cares

Kimberly A. Gatto

Enslow Elementary

an imprint of

Enslow Publishers, Inc.

40 Industrial Road
Box 398
Berkeley Heights, NJ 07922
USA

http://www.enslow.com

Enslow Elementary, an imprint of Enslow Publishers, Inc.

Enslow Elementary® is a registered trademark of Enslow Publishers, Inc.

Library of Congress Cataloging-in-Publication Data

Gatto, Kimberly
  Kevin Garnett : a basketball star who cares / Kimberly A. Gatto.
    p. cm. — (Sports stars who care)
  Includes bibliographical references and index.
  Summary: "A biography of basketball star Kevin Garnett,
highlighting his charitable work"—Provided by publisher.
  ISBN 978-0-7660-3772-4
  1. Garnett, Kevin, 1976—Juvenile literature. 2. Basketball players--
United States—Biography—Juvenile literature. 3. Generosity—Juvenile literature. I. Title.
  GV884.G3G38 2011
  796.323092—dc22
  [B]
                        2010008681

122010 Lake Book Manufacturing, Inc., Melrose Park, IL

Printed in the United States of America

10 9 8 7 6 5 4 3 2 1

Illustration Credits: AP/Wide World Photos

Cover Illustration: AP/Wide World Photos

Contents

Introduction

Kevin Garnett has many nicknames. He has been called "the Big Ticket," "the Kid," and "the Franchise." But he is probably best known by his initials, "KG."

Garnett is a power forward. He plays for the Boston Celtics in the National Basketball Association (NBA). Power forwards usually play close to the basket. That is called "the low post." Power forwards grab a lot of rebounds. A typical NBA power forward is 6 feet 8 inches or taller. Kevin Garnett is 6 feet 11 inches.

Garnett is one of the best defensive players in the NBA. Defense keeps the other team from scoring. To score points, players must put the ball through the hoop. A good defender will block the ball. He may force the player to shoot from farther away. He may also steal the ball.

Garnett is an intense player. He gets his

teammates excited to play. He sometimes jumps up and down and waves his arms before games. He often thumps his fist against his chest. Garnett also sets a good example for others to follow. His motto is "anything is possible."

"It's the energy he has, he gives you energy just looking at him," said Garnett's teammate, Glen Davis. "That's what I love about Kevin—he's a wonderful guy and a competitor."

Kevin Garnett guards an opposing player during a playoff game.

The Boston Celtics have a successful history. They have won more NBA championships than any other team. The Celtics won 11 titles in the 1950s and 1960s. They won 5 more in the 1970s and 1980s. After that, the team began to struggle. By 2007, the Celtics were on a

Chapter 1

The Big Ticket

losing streak. They only won 24 games during the entire season.

Boston is a huge sports town. Fans are very passionate about their teams. By the mid-2000s, they had good reason to be. The Boston Red Sox had won the World Series. And the New England Patriots had won three Super Bowls. But the Celtics, known for their green-and-white uniforms, were a disappointment.

Some Boston fans remembered how good "the Green" used to be. They talked about Celtic Pride, a sense of respect and loyalty for the team. Younger fans had heard stories of how great the old Celtics were. Young or old, the fans shared a common goal. They wanted the Celtics to win again.

The 2007 Celtics were led by their captain, five-time all-star Paul Pierce. He scored a lot of points and never gave up. But most of the other Celtics were not great players. Many were young and just starting out. Pierce needed some veteran

Garnett drives
to the hoop!

teammates to help him win games. The Celtics owners decided to rebuild the team.

In the summer of 2007, the Celtics made a deal with the Seattle SuperSonics. They picked up Ray Allen, a seven-time all-star guard. Then the Celtics made a trade with the Minnesota Timberwolves. The Celtics got superstar Kevin Garnett. In return, the Celtics traded five players to the Timberwolves. They also traded two draft picks and paid some cash. It was the biggest trade for one player in NBA history.

Garnett was happy to sign with the Celtics. He was proud to wear the green uniform. He knew that the fans and media had high expectations. But that just made Garnett more excited. That night, he said, "It's like being in a Lamborghini doing 200 (miles per hour) with your head stuck out the window. It's been like a whirlwind [the last 72 hours]."

Sportswriters began calling Garnett, Pierce, and Allen "the Big Three." Back in the 1980s, the Celtics had another Big Three: Larry Bird, Kevin

Garnett slams a monster dunk!

McHale, and Robert Parish. These players had led the Celtics to three world titles. Fans hoped that the new Big Three would bring glory back to Boston. They would have to wait and see.

Kevin Maurice Garnett was born on May 19, 1976. He has an older sister, Sonya, and a younger sister, Ashley. The family lived in Mauldin, a small town in South Carolina. The Garnett children were raised by their mother, Shirley. She worked as a hairstylist to support the family.

Chapter 2

Early Years

As a child, Kevin was taller than most of his friends. He was good at sports, especially basketball. His favorite player was Earvin "Magic" Johnson of the Los Angeles Lakers.

"All [Kevin] did was talk about basketball," said Garnett's friend, Baron "Bear" Franks. "And every time you saw him, he had a ball. Sun up. Sun down. Up and down the street. All day long."

Kevin worked hard to improve his game. He practiced a lot. Sometimes he would sneak out to nearby Springfield Park when his mom was not looking. He would shoot baskets for hours, often until well after dark. At other times he practiced at a gym called the Armory. This gym had no air conditioning. It was so hot at times that people called it "the Oven."

Kevin did not care how hot it was inside or outside. Playing basketball made him feel good wherever he was. He later said, "When I didn't have a friend, when I was lonely . . . If things weren't going right, I could make a basket and feel better."

Garnett shoots over Larry Hughes of the New York Knicks.

By the time he reached high school, Garnett was the best basketball player in South Carolina. He played for three years on the Mauldin Mavericks high school team. Until Kevin joined the team, the Mavericks had never posted a winning record. Kevin quickly changed that. In his first season, he helped the Mavericks win 19 games. He also led them to the state's final four championship.

In his junior year, Kevin was named "Mr. Basketball" for the state of South Carolina. He was the first junior in the history of the state to earn that honor. People came from all over to watch Kevin play. Kids even asked for his autograph. Kevin's coach, Duke Fisher, remembered, "He got up for big games. He made everybody else play to a different level. Everybody, I think, played better when he was in there."

Kevin Garnett dribbles around an opposing player.

Around this time, Kevin started his trademark of wearing a rubber band around his wrist or ankle. Many of the other kids had nice watches or jewelry. Kevin could not afford these things. He decided to wear a rubber band instead. "The rubber band thing came from just a concept, just something in my head," Kevin later said. "I didn't have any braces or anything to wear like that, so I would just throw a rubber band on it."

Before his senior year, Kevin's family moved to Chicago, Illinois. Kevin attended the Farragut Career Academy, which had a great basketball program. That season, he averaged 25.2 points, 17.9 rebounds, 6.7 assists, and 6.5 blocks. He was named "Mr. Basketball" for the state of Illinois. He was also Most Outstanding Player at the 1995 McDonald's All-American Game. "Chicago gave me a different flair," Garnett later said. "Now that I look back on it, I was a young boy turning into a man. It was definitely a grow-up kind of year for me."

Kevin did not really like school. But his mother wanted him to go to college. She knew it was important. And Kevin had planned on doing so. "My plan was to do four years of college, not just for the basketball but for the education part, to better myself that way," he later said.

Chapter 3

"The Kid"

A young Kevin Garnett handles the ball during his rookie year in Minnesota in 1995.

Kevin was having trouble passing the ACT test, which would have made him eligible to play in college. He would not be able to play in college that year. So Kevin made an unusual choice. He decided to enter the NBA draft right after high school. The draft is the way teams pick their newest young players each year.

Usually, players are around twenty-two years old when they enter the draft. Many have gone to college for four years. Playing in college helps athletes get ready for the NBA. Kevin was only eighteen and had not gone to college. But his skills were better than many older players. Teams noticed how he could score and block shots. One of these teams was the Minnesota Timberwolves.

The Timberwolves were a struggling team. They had won only 21 games in 1995. The team needed a strong leader who could rebound and score. They hoped that Kevin would be the one to turn the team around.

The Timberwolves chose Kevin as their first-round pick in the draft. He was chosen fifth overall. He was the first NBA player in more than twenty years to be drafted straight from high school. Because of his age, the media nicknamed him "the Kid."

During his rookie season, Kevin started out on the bench. He only played when the starters needed a rest. Later in the year, the Timberwolves got a new coach, Flip Saunders. The new coach liked Kevin and gave him more playing time. By

Even as a nineteen-year-old rookie, Garnett was a great shot blocker.

the end of the year he had averaged 10.4 points and 6.3 rebounds per game.

The following season, Garnett became a starter. People began to really notice what he could do. In two separate games, Garnett blocked eight shots. He also helped lead the Timberwolves to a 40–42 record. They made the playoffs for the first time in team history. Garnett also played in the All-Star Game that season. He was the youngest All-Star starter since 1980. The previous record had been set by his idol, Magic Johnson.

During the 1997–98 season, Kevin Garnett signed a new contract. He would play with the Timberwolves for the next six seasons. The contract was worth $126 million. It was the most ever for an NBA player. "The Kid" had become the highest paid star in the NBA.

Garnett flies through the air during a game against the Los Angeles Lakers in 1999.

In 2000, Garnett helped lead Team USA to a gold medal at the Summer Olympics. By this time he had become a superstar. In the 2001–02 NBA season, Garnett averaged 21.2 points, 12.1 rebounds, 5.2 assists, 1.6 blocks, and 1.2 steals per game. The next year he had even

Chapter 4

Pro Player

higher stats. He placed second in the league's MVP voting, behind Tim Duncan of the San Antonio Spurs.

Things began to look even better for Garnett and his team during the 2003–04 season. The Timberwolves got two new players, Latrell Sprewell and Sam Cassell. These players could help the team win more games.

The addition of Sprewell and Cassell helped. Together with Garnett, they were the highest scoring trio in the NBA. The Timberwolves made it to the Western Conference Semifinals for the first time. Garnett was named MVP of the league for the 2003–04 season. In the summer of 2004, Garnett married his longtime girlfriend, Brandi Padilla.

By the next season, the Timberwolves began having problems. Sprewell and Cassell became upset with their contracts. Both players eventually left the team. Garnett tried his hardest to help the team win. But it was difficult. The Timberwolves ended the 2005–06 season with a record of 33–49 and did not make the playoffs.

The next season brought even more disappointment to Garnett and the fans. The team kept losing games. Garnett began to grow frustrated. Minnesota's owners started to think it was time to rebuild with young players. To do so they would not be able to pay

Garnett shoots a layup while playing for Team USA.

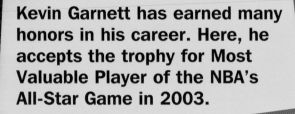

Kevin Garnett has earned many honors in his career. Here, he accepts the trophy for Most Valuable Player of the NBA's All-Star Game in 2003.

Kevin Garnett's big salary. They would have to trade him to another team.

At first, Garnett did not like the idea of being traded. The star was loyal to his team even though they were not winning. But he decided to listen to the trade offer made by the Boston Celtics. He liked their captain, Paul Pierce. He also liked their newest player, Ray Allen. Garnett had played with Allen on the Olympic team in 2000.

On July 31, 2007, Garnett was traded to the Celtics. He quickly bonded with Paul Pierce and

Kevin Garnett stands between new teammates Paul Pierce (left) and Ray Allen (right) during a press conference shortly after he was traded to the Celtics.

Ray Allen to form the Celtics new "Big Three." Rajon Rondo, at guard, and Kendrick Perkins, at center, completed the starting five.

The team began the season with a bang, winning their first eight games. By midseason, they had a record of 41–9. The Celtics beat strong teams like the Los Angeles Lakers and the San Antonio Spurs. Suddenly, the Celtics had become a strong force in the NBA. Fans began wearing green and white again. All home games were sold out. It was the beginning of a new era.

Paul Pierce said about Garnett, "The whole face of Celtics nation turned around when the trade happened with this guy."

Garnett made the NBA All-Star team for the eleventh straight year. The All-Star teams are decided by the votes of the fans. Garnett received more votes than any other player. In April 2008, Garnett had another reason to be excited. He and his wife, Brandi, welcomed a baby girl. It seemed that Garnett's life could not get any better.

The Celtics finished the 2007–08 regular season with 66 wins. It was the best turnaround by any team in NBA history. It was also the best record in the NBA. This earned them home-court advantage for the playoffs. It was hard to believe that the team had won only 24 games the previous year.

Chapter 5

Champion

Many felt that the Celtics would just keep on winning. But the playoffs would be a challenge. There would be more pressure on the players. They were a very talented team. But none of the "Big Three" had ever played in the NBA Finals. Other teams, such as the Los Angeles Lakers and the Detroit Pistons, had recently won championships. They would be tough to beat.

The NBA playoffs have several rounds. In each round, a team must win four games out of seven to move on. Sometimes a team will win four straight games. At other times, a series may go the distance and last seven games.

The Celtics began the playoffs against the Atlanta Hawks. The Hawks were a young team. Many fans felt that the Celtics would beat them easily. As expected, the Celtics won the first two games in Boston. Then they headed to Atlanta for two games.

The Celtics were caught off guard in Atlanta. The Hawks fans cheered wildly for their team. They booed at the Celtics. That energy helped the

A defender tries to block Garnett as he puts up a shot for his new team.

Hawks, as they won, 102–93. Then the Hawks won the next game, 97–92. The Celtics were playing sloppy basketball. They were turning the ball over and letting the Hawks score easy baskets. The mighty Celtics seemed to have lost their confidence.

The series returned to Boston for Game 5. At home, the Celtics once again looked like champions. They won easily. But back in Atlanta for Game 6, they once again fell apart. It was now back to Boston for the final game with the series even at 3–3. Garnett was so nervous that he could not sleep. "I haven't slept," he later said. "I've been up for nearly 24 hours thinking about Game 6 and the things we [needed] to do."

Garnett had to find a way to motivate the team. He had an idea. He usually ate peanut butter and jelly sandwiches before each game. It had become a ritual for him. So he decided to bring sandwiches to the locker room and share them with his teammates. It became a new Celtic tradition.

Garnett's plan seemed to work. The Celtics beat the Hawks by 34 points in Game 7. Garnett had 18 points and 11 rebounds. Now it was time to face LeBron James and the Cleveland Cavaliers. LeBron, often known by his nickname "King James," is one of the youngest superstars in the NBA. He is also one of the best. It is difficult to keep King James from scoring.

Just as the Hawks did, the Cavaliers tested the Celtics. Once again, the Celtics won at home but were unable to win on the road. The series went seven games, with the Celtics winning the series in Game 7 at home. They would move on to the next round. But there was a problem. The Celtics had still not won a game on the road.

The next series would determine the Eastern Conference champions. If the Celtics could win this round, they would play in the NBA Finals. Garnett's lifelong dream was becoming a reality.

The Celtics would face the Detroit Pistons in the Eastern Conference Finals. The Pistons were another tough team. After Boston won Game 1,

Garnett dunks over Pau Gasol of the Los Angeles Lakers during the 2008 NBA Finals.

Detroit stunned the Celtics by beating them at home in Game 2 of the series. It was the first time in the playoffs that the Celtics had lost at home. Now they would have to win on the road to take the series.

Garnett tried his best to keep the team motivated. He told them he knew they could win. And it worked. Thanks to Garnett's great defense, the Celtics won Game 3 in Detroit by a score of 94–80. They won another game on the road to win the series in six games. The Celtics were headed to the NBA Finals for the first time in twenty-one years!

In the finals, the Celtics would face their biggest rivals, the Los Angeles Lakers. Like the Celtics, the Lakers are a famous team. They have won many NBA titles. In 2008 the Lakers were led by superstar Kobe Bryant. Boston fans were excited by the renewed rivalry with the Lakers. Many wore T-shirts that said, "Beat LA."

Going into the finals, the Celtics had beaten the Lakers both times they met that season. But the Lakers had since acquired a new seven-foot center, Pau Gasol. Along with Kobe Bryant, Gasol and the Lakers would be tough to stop.

The Celtics started the series strong. They won the first two games at home. The Lakers came back tough in Game 3 on their home court. In Game 4, the Celtics were down by 24 points in the first half but came back to win. They only had to win one more game and they would be the NBA Champions.

The Lakers fought back in Game 5 and won, 103–98. Now it was back to Boston. Garnett and the Celtics were determined to win at home for the fans. They led Game 6 from start to finish, winning, 131–92. The Celtics had brought NBA glory back to Boston. Garnett was overcome with emotion. Everything he had worked for his entire career had paid off. After the game, he shouted his motto, "Anything is possible!" He had proven that was true.

On October 31, 2008, Kevin Garnett watched with pride as the championship banner was raised to the rafters at the TD Garden. He received the ring he had been dreaming of for years, and proved that success is possible with hard work and believing in yourself.

Garnett, Allen, and Pierce (left to right) pose with the 2008 championship trophy after the Celtics beat the Lakers in the NBA Finals.

Kevin Garnett loves the game of basketball. On the court, he is focused on winning. But he also knows that there are more important things in life. When he is not playing basketball, Garnett spends a lot of time helping others.

Chapter 6

Making a Difference

In August 2005, Hurricane Katrina hit the Gulf Coast of the United States. Many people were killed. Thousands of buildings were destroyed. Folks were injured and hungry. Many had no place to live.

Garnett saw TV coverage about the hurricane and its effects on the people. It upset him to see people without homes. He kept thinking about how lucky he was. So Garnett decided he would help out.

Talk show host Oprah Winfrey was leading a mission to build new homes for the people hit by Hurricane Katrina. Garnett pledged to help out by donating money to build one new home each month for the next two years. All in all, Garnett donated more than $1.2 million. That built twenty-four new homes.

"I heard [Oprah's message] about what people could do individually to help those affected by Hurricane Katrina, and it made me think about what I could do," Garnett later said. "Through

this project we are directly helping people who need it the most."

Garnett also took part in the NBA Players Hurricane Relief Game in Houston, Texas. Each player donated at least ten thousand dollars to buy supplies for the victims of the hurricane. He even hosted families in his suite at the Target Center in Minnesota.

A young child experiences a slam dunk while Garnett holds him up to the basket. This was during a charity game to help the victims of Hurricane Katrina.

Garnett donated the sneakers he wore during the 2008 NBA Finals to a local charity for auctioning.

Garnett continued his good works to help people. He visited sick children in hospitals. He helped hand out turkey dinners to needy families at Thanksgiving. Garnett did not do these things for praise. But it was tough for others not to notice how much he was doing. In 2006, the Professional Basketball Writers Association presented Garnett with the J. Walter Kennedy Citizenship Award. This award honors an NBA player or coach for outstanding community service.

Garnett also does a lot to inspire kids and teens. Through his 4XL Foundation, he helps teens prepare for careers in business. He also takes part in many charity events. Recently, Garnett played in a charity bowling tournament hosted by his teammate Paul Pierce. This event raised money for needy kids. He also donated his NBA Finals sneakers to be auctioned off for a local charity.

Many sports stars do charitable works so others will see them. They want their pictures taken. But Garnett does his charity work outside of the spotlight. He simply likes to help others.

"I am happy that I can help make a difference in the communities," he said, "and blessed to be in the position where I am able to lend support. Hopefully, this will encourage others to do the same."

Career Statistics

NBA

SEASON	TEAM	GP	FG%	REB	AST	STL	BLK	PTS	AVG
1995–1996	Minnesota	80	49.1	501	145	86	131	835	10.4
1996–1997	Minnesota	77	49.9	618	236	105	163	1,309	17.0
1997–1998	Minnesota	82	49.1	786	348	139	150	1,518	18.5
1998–1999	Minnesota	47	46.0	489	202	78	83	977	20.8
1999–2000	Minnesota	81	49.7	956	401	120	126	1,857	22.9
2000–2001	Minnesota	81	47.7	921	401	111	145	1,784	22.0
2001–2002	Minnesota	81	47.0	981	422	96	126	1,714	21.2
2002–2003	Minnesota	82	50.2	1,102	495	113	129	1,883	23.0
2003–2004	Minnesota	82	49.9	1,139	409	120	178	1,987	24.2
2004–2005	Minnesota	82	50.2	1,108	466	121	112	1,817	22.2
2005–2006	Minnesota	76	52.6	966	308	104	107	1,656	21.8
2006–2007	Minnesota	76	47.6	975	313	89	126	1,704	22.4
2007–2008	Boston	71	53.9	655	244	100	89	1,337	18.8
2008–2009	Boston	57	53.1	485	144	63	68	899	15.8
2009–2010	Boston	69	52.1	506	185	68	57	990	14.3
TOTALS		1,124	49.7	12,188	4,719	1,513	1,790	22,267	19.8

GP=Games Played   REB=Rebounds   STL=Steals PTS= Points
FG%=Field Goal Percentage   AST=Assists   BLK=Blocks AVG= Average

Where to Write

Kevin Garnett
c/o Boston Celtics
226 Causeway Street
Fourth Floor
Boston, MA 02114

Words to Know

assist—The act of passing the ball to a teammate so that he can score.

center—Usually the tallest person on a team, the center blocks shots and plays close to the basket.

culture—The attitude or behavior of a group.

defense—The act of stopping the other team from scoring.

guard—Either of two players who play farthest from the basket. A point guard is responsible for bringing the ball up the court and passing it to open players for scoring.

home-court advantage—The idea that a team plays better at its own court.

MVP—The person who receives the Most Valuable Player award.

NBA Finals—The championship series of the National Basketball Association.

rebound—The act of taking the ball after a missed shot.

starter—One of the five key players on a basketball team. Starters begin the game and usually have the most playing time.

trademark—Something that is associated with a certain person or thing.

veteran—A player with years of experience.

Books

Doeden, Matt. *The World's Greatest Basketball Players.* Mankato, Minn.: Capstone Press, 2010.

Edwards, Ethan. *Meet Kevin Garnett: Basketball's Big Ticket.* New York: PowerKids Press, 2009.

Woods, Mark. *Basketball Legends.* New York: Crabtree Pub. Co., 2009.

Internet Addresses

Kevin Garnett Info Page, NBA.com
http://www.nba.com/playerfile/kevin_garnett/

SIKids.com (*Sports Illustrated*)
http://www.sikids.com/

Official Kevin Garnett Web Site
http://www.kevingarnett.com/